MINERVA LOUISE
at School

Janet Morgan Stoeke

PUFFIN BOOKS

For my mom and dad with love.

PUFFIN BOOKS
Published by the Penguin Group
Penguin Putnam Books for Young Readers, 345 Hudson Street, New York, New York 10014, U.S.A.
Penguin Books Ltd, 27 Wrights Lane, London W8 5TZ, England
Penguin Books Australia Ltd, Ringwood, Victoria, Australia
Penguin Books Canada Ltd, 10 Alcorn Avenue, Toronto, Ontario, Canada M4V 3B2
Penguin Books (N.Z.) Ltd, 182-190 Wairau Road, Auckland 10, New Zealand

Penguin Books Ltd, Registered Offices: Harmondsworth, Middlesex, England

First published in the United States of America by Dutton Children's Books,
a member of Penguin Putnam Inc., 1996
Published by Puffin Books, a member of Penguin Putnam Books for Young Readers, 1999

10 9 8 7 6 5 4 3 2 1

Copyright © Janet Morgan Stoeke, 1996

THE LIBRARY OF CONGRESS HAS CATALOGED THE DUTTON EDITION AS FOLLOWS:
Stoeke, Janet Morgan.
Minerva Louise at school/Janet Morgan Stoeke.
[author and illustrator].—1st ed.
p. cm.
Summary: Out for an early morning walk, a chicken wanders into a school
that she mistakes for a fancy barn.
ISBN 0-525-45494-2
[1. Schools—Fiction. 2. Chickens—Fiction.] I. Title.
PZ7.S869Mk 1996 [E]—dc20 95-52173 CIP AC

Puffin Books ISBN 0-14-056287-7

Printed in the United States of America

One morning, Minerva Louise woke up before everyone else.

It was a beautiful morning, so she decided
to go for a walk through the tall grass.

She walked on and on.

Oh, look! A big, fancy barn,
thought Minerva Louise.

She watched the farmer hang
his laundry out to dry . . .

. . . and she noticed that he had
left the door open.

So many stalls! There must be
all kinds of animals here.

Here are milking stools for the cows

and a pen for the pigs.

Oh, a bucket, too. It must be
for feeding the chickens.

Nesting boxes! How wonderful!

Look at them all. And each one
is decorated differently.

This one is all done up with ribbons.

And this one is lined with fur.

Oh my goodness, there's an EGG in this one!

But where is his mother? He'll get cold.

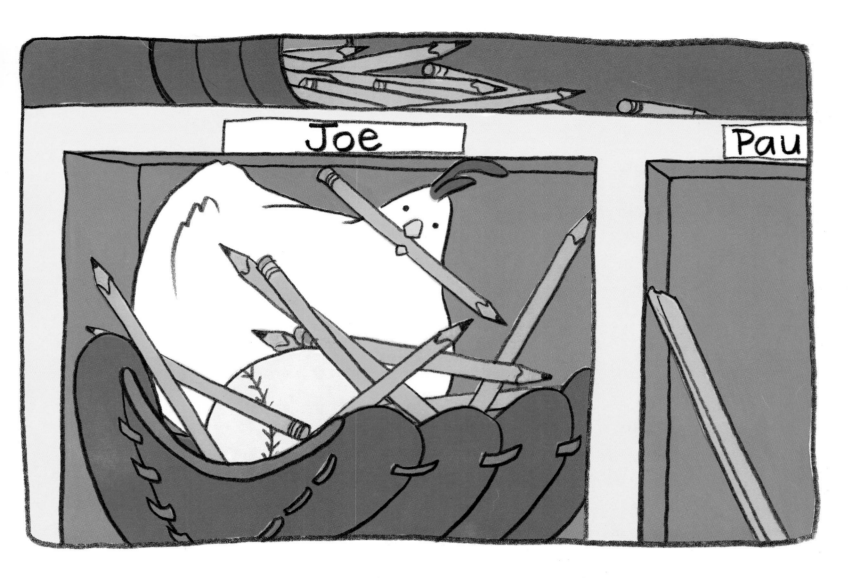

Well, this hay will keep you warm.

I'm sure the animals are around here somewhere. But I have to go home now.

Minerva Louise hurried home
through the tall grass.

She had some work to do.

But she knew she'd go back to the
fancy barn some day . . .

because it was such a wonderful
place to get new ideas.